The Video Shop Sparrow

story by

JOY COWLEY

illustrated by

GAVIN BISHOP

BOYDS MILLS PRESS

First published in 1999 by
Mallinson Rendel Publishers Ltd, Wellington, New Zealand.

Published by Caroline House
Boyds Mills Press
A Highlights Company
815 Church Street
Honesdale, Pennsylvania 18431
Printed in China

Cataloging-in-Publication Data
available upon request from publisher.

Library of Congress Catalog Card Number: LC 99-67091

ISBN 1-56397-826-1

First U.S. edition, 1999

10 9 8 7 6 5 4 3 2 1

On New Year's Day,
George and Harry
went to town
to return the video
they had rented.

The video shop was closed.
On the door was a notice,
WILL REOPEN JANUARY 13
and under the notice was a flap
like the mouth of a letterbox.
George pushed the video
under the flap and it fell clunk
into the bag on the other side.

Harry, who had his nose pressed hard
against the glass window, said,
"Hey George! Look! A sparrow!
It's flying around the shop."

The restaurant across the street
was open.
"Can I get something for you?"
asked the woman
who was wiping the tables.

"There's a sparrow in the video shop,"
said George. "It's locked in."
"The shop won't open again
for nearly two weeks," said Harry.

George said, "Maybe the video man
could come and open the door.
Do you know where he lives?"

The woman shook her head.
"He's gone on vacation.
But don't worry kids.
It's only a sparrow.
Plenty more where that came from."

George and Harry rushed home to tell their mother and father about the video shop sparrow.

Their father knew the video man.
He tried to call him but all he got
was an answering machine.

"He's gone all right,"
their father said.

"We'll have to rescue it,"
said George.

His father shook his head.
"Forget it," he said.
"Sparrows aren't exactly
an endangered species."

That afternoon, the boys went back to the video shop.
The sparrow was now in the window.
It was flying up and down the glass, trying to get out.

When the sparrow saw George and Harry
it stopped flying.
Harry said,
"It's got a special look in its eye.
It knows we are trying to rescue it."

George turned to his brother.
"Who rescues people?" he said.
"Who can bust down locked doors
to get inside places?"

"I know! I know!" shouted Harry.

Then George and Harry went
as fast as they could to the police station.

"The video shop!" cried George.
"It's an emergency! It's locked inside.
Going to d-d-d-die."

The policeman stood up.
"Are you trying to tell me
someone's in trouble in the video shop?"

The boys nodded and Harry said,
"It's flying in the window and the shop
doesn't open until January 13th."
"Flying?" the man stopped.
"Are we talking about a bird?"
"A sparrow," George said.
"Please! You can bust down the door!"

The policeman sat down again.
He said, "Last night was New Year's Eve.
On New Year's Eve I don't get much sleep.
Now buzz off, both of you, before you find out
what I can be like when I'm tired."
"But what about the sparrow?" asked George.

"It can tweet in bird heaven," the policeman said.

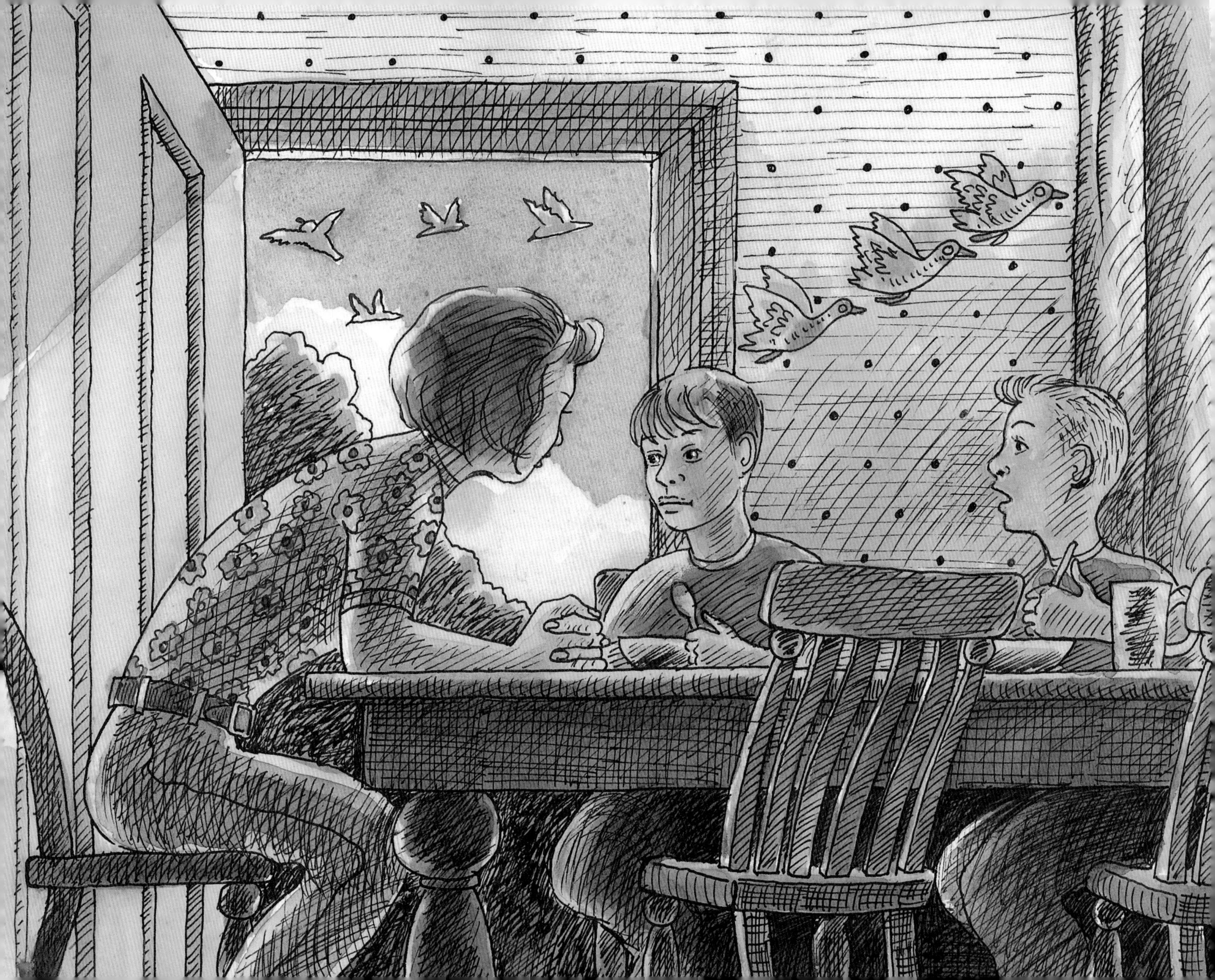

The next day,
their mother talked to them about death.
"Everyone dies," she said. "That's life.
Great-grandpa died. The cat died.
Don't worry about it. There are
millions of sparrows in the world."

"It's not dead yet," said Harry,
mashing his cornflakes into the milk.
"It's waiting for us to rescue it."

"Why don't you take some bread out
to feed the sparrows in the garden?"
said their father.

"What good will that do?" asked George.

His father smiled.
"It will make you realize
that sparrows are like ants.
One more or less
doesn't matter all that much."

The sparrow in the video shop
was no longer flying.
It crouched on a shelf,
its feathers ruffled.
It still had a special look in its eye.

George and Harry sat in the gutter
and tried to think of something.

"I reckon it will be dead by tomorrow,"
Harry said.

George didn't want to think about that.
"Dad always says if you want a job done,
you have to go to the top," he said.
"Who do you reckon
is the top in this town?
Who is the big boss?
Mrs. McKenzie the mayor!"

A man answered the door
of Mrs. McKenzie's house.
"I'm sorry," he said to the boys.
"You can't see the mayor.
She's having a press conference
with people from four newspapers."

"We'll wait till she's finished,"
said George, and they sat
on the steps.

Mrs. McKenzie must have seen them
because she came out
and asked why they were there.

George told her about the sparrow.

Mrs. McKenzie looked
at all the newspaper people.
Then she smiled a big warm smile.
"Forget about the road taxes," she said.
"Forget about the problems
with the sewer system.
Is it a story you want?
Ladies and gentlemen, come with me
and I will give you a story."

Mrs. McKenzie knew just about everyone,
including a security guard who had several bunches of keys.

They all went to the back of the video shop
and the guard opened the door.

Harry and George ran in.
They went straight to the front window.

The sparrow was lying on the floor and it was still alive.

George picked it up in both hands.
He could feel its heart beating
against his fingers.

He and Harry would have let it go
right there and then.
But Mrs. McKenzie wanted a photo first.
George had to shelter the sparrow
while the cameras went flash, flash, flash,
and Mrs. McKenzie told
the newspaper people
that no job was too small
for a caring mayor.

Then George was able to open his hands.

For a while the bird lay on his palm,
its heart ticking like a tiny watch.
George blew gently on it.

The sparrow opened its eyes,
shook its feathers a little
and gave him that special trusting look.
Then it spread its wings and fluttered
and it leapt right into the air.

George thought it might fall,
but it flew over the fence
and in a moment, was gone.

Their mother shook her head.
"I never know what you two
are going to do next."

Their father showed them
their photo in the newspaper
with Mrs. McKenzie and the sparrow.

"She's a very nice lady," said George.

"And very smart," said his father.

Above the photo were the words,
THE CHAMPION OF
SPARROWS AND CHILDREN.

That afternoon, George and Harry
fed bread to the sparrows in the garden.
They thought that their bird
might have been there, too,
but it was hard to tell, because now,
every sparrow they saw
had that special trusting look.